this book

BELONGS

to

Mac and Bob's

Friend

D0488572

For Mum, Dad and Susan, lots of love x
Special thanks once again to Vivian French, Dave Gray and Paul Croan – AW

Enormous gratitude for all the support received on this Mac and Bob journey – DS

Published by Little Door Books 2015
This edition published 2015

ISBN: 978-0-9927520-1-9

Text copyright © Alan Windram 2015
Illustrations copyright © David Sutton 2015

A CIP catalogue record for this book is available from the British Library.

All songs written by Alan Windram - copyright control 2015
(Except 'Hokey Cokey' - traditional)

Little Door Books

mail@littledoorbooks.co.uk
www.littledoorbooks.co.uk
www.macandbob.co.uk

Printed in China

Mac and Bob

the Party Problem

Written by

ALAN Windram

illustrated by

DAVE SUTTON

Little Door Books

Mac and Bob were sitting in the kitchen enjoying raspberry jam sandwiches and a cup of tea, when all of a sudden there was a noise at the door.

"I wonder what that is?" said Mac.

Bob scampered into the hall to find a large envelope lying on the door mat.

They opened the envelope,
and as they did, lots of sparkly stars, party poppers
and streamers jumped out,
along with a brightly coloured invitation to a

PARTY

"wowee!" cried Mac.

"I love parties - lots of food, lots of music, lots of dancing... and lots more food!"

"I love food and music, and dancing too!" said Bob.

So Mac gathered up all his clothes,
which were very dirty from working on the farm.

He even took off the ones he had on.

Bob put them all into the washing machine
and he watched as the clothes went round and round, and round and round again.

Mac sat in his underwear with a big smile on his face and another large cup of tea.

Looking out of the window, Mac noticed the trees
swaying backwards and forwards.
It was getting very windy.

"Brilliant," he said,
"everything is going so well.
All my clothes will dry really
quickly in this wind."

As soon as the washing was done, Bob put Mac's clothes in a basket and they went outside to hang them up on the washing line.

Mac was still in his underwear, but he was in such a good mood he started to dance and sing his washing-day song.

"Pick up a peg and put it on your pants, hang them on the line and watch them dance!

Dance to the left and dance to the right,

soon they'll be dry and clean and bright!!"

As he sang, Mac hung up all his washing.

Bob laughed and laughed as he watched Mac, dressed in only his underwear and wellies, dance his way back into the house.

Together they sat by the fire and had another jam sandwich.

Outside, the wind was getting stronger and stronger, blowing the trees and bushes backwards and forwards, to the left and to the right.

When Mac and Bob looked
out of the window,
all of his clothes had

GONE!

Oh, dear!

They ran outside.
Only the pegs were left on the washing line.

"Bob, Bob," Mac shouted,
"what are we going to do?

All my clothes have blown away!"

Bob started running around the farm looking for the missing clothes.

In the barn, he found Mac's dungarees wrapped around the cow.

Mac began looking for his clothes
along the lane, when he saw Mr Green
the postman cycling towards him.

He realised he was still in his underwear,
so he quickly jumped into the bushes
and waited until Mr Green had passed by.

In the yard, the chickens were happily clucking around with Mac's, now very dirty, socks on their heads.

"I think this colour really suits me," said the pig.

Further up the lane, Bob found the pig rolling in the mud with Mac's shirt on its back.

"Oh dear! Everything is dirty again."

On his way to the field, Mac had to hide under the bridge to avoid Mrs Flower the baker...

and then jump behind the tractor when Polly and Poppy Brown came skipping down the road.

By now, even the underwear that Mac had on was dirty.

"Oh dear," said Mac, "what am I going to do?"

He sat down on a bucket and watched as Gilbert the horse came trotting down the field wearing Mac's best jacket on his back and his underpants on his head.

"Do you like my new look?" said Gilbert, "It came by air-mail!"

Once Bob had gathered up all the very dirty clothes, he found Mac looking very sad.

"What am I going to wear now, Bob?" he sighed.

"All my clothes are dirty again and it's nearly time for the party."

Suddenly, Bob spotted something in the distance.

He told Mac his great idea.

"WOWEE! Bob, that's BRILLIANT!" said Mac.

"Let's do it!"

Standing tall in the middle of the field was the old scarecrow, who was wearing the only clean clothes on the farm.

"What an amazing idea, Bob!"

said Mac, as they made their way to the village hall for the party.

Mac was wearing the scarecrow's old clothes, with brightly coloured patches on his elbows and knees, and straw sticking out everywhere.

And when they arrived, they opened the door to find that it wasn't just any old party ...

It was a **fancy dress party!**

What a great night they had,

with music and dancing,

and lots

and lots

of food.

Afterwards, Mac and Bob skipped along the road to the farmhouse carrying their prize for the best dressed scarecrow at the party.

WINNER! BEST FANCY DRESS COSTUME

"I love parties," said Mac. "especially fancy dress parties."

Bob smiled and said: "So do I Mac, so do I."

THE END